Merry Christmas, TINY!

by Cari Meister

illustrated by Rich Davis

Penguin Workshop

For Koki—CM

To Scott,
moving the barge from Memphis
to New Orleans with you taught
me invaluable secrets. Thank you—RD

PENGUIN WORKSHOP
An Imprint of Penguin Random House LLC, New York

Text copyright © 2020 by Cari Meister. Illustrations copyright © 2020 by Richard D. Davis. All rights reserved.
Published by Penguin Workshop, an imprint of Penguin Random House LLC, New York.
PENGUIN and PENGUIN WORKSHOP are trademarks of Penguin Books Ltd, and the
W colophon is a registered trademark of Penguin Random House LLC.
Manufactured in China.

Visit us online at www.penguinrandomhouse.com.

Library of Congress Cataloging-in-Publication Data is available upon request.

ISBN 9780593097373 (pbk)   10 9 8 7 6 5 4 3 2 1
ISBN 9780593097380 (hc)   10 9 8 7 6 5 4 3 2 1

It's Christmas Eve! Tiny and I are finishing a few last-minute things.

"Should we hang up the stockings first or wrap presents?" I ask Tiny.

It looks like Tiny wants to hang up the stockings.

Wait a minute, Tiny!

Crash!

"Are you okay?" I ask Tiny.

Let me help. There! They are perfect.

We are just about to wrap the last few presents when the doorbell rings.

Ding-dong.

It's carolers!

Tiny wants to join them.

Wait, Tiny. It looks cold outside.

Let's get our warm stuff.

There. All set!

"Ruff!" says Tiny.

Whoops—sorry!

We sing a lot of songs, like "We Wish You a Merry Christmas" and "We Three Kings."

It starts to snow harder. I have never seen so much snow!

At the senior center, they invite me and Tiny inside to warm up.

Tiny hardly fits!

When he knocks
over the giant Santa,
the nurse gets mad.
I tell her Tiny is sorry.
She says he should
wait outside.

But the seniors
love Tiny, so he
gets to stay.

We help the seniors make a long popcorn chain.
It is going really well, until . . .

Tiny, stop!

The nurse is angry again and tells us to leave, but the seniors don't want Tiny to go. They tell the nurse that everyone makes mistakes.

The nurse agrees to let us stay—but we only have one more chance.

Now it is time to decorate cookies. I sit down and start decorating one, too. That's when I notice Tiny is not next to me.

Where is he?

Oh no!

That's not for you, Tiny!

But I'm too late. The Christmas cake display is ruined.

This time the nurse
tells us that it's time
for us to go home.

Tiny and I get
ready to leave.

It's a winter wonderland outside!

A man in an elf costume runs up the sidewalk.

"Sorry, folks," he says. "We won't be able to bring in the Christmas tree tonight. I was driving back from the tree farm, with the tree in the back of my truck, when the truck broke down. We'll have to wait until morning."

"But it's Christmas Eve," says a woman wearing jingle bells around her neck.

"There has to be another way to get it here," someone else says.

Tiny barks.

Yes! That's it! Tiny and I can go get the tree!

The nurse isn't sure. The elf shrugs. He says his truck is just a few blocks away.

We decide we have to try. The woman with the
jingle bells lets us borrow them so people can hear
us coming. Another man gives us a giant flashlight.
The nurse lends us her sled. Soon, we are ready.

Let's go, Tiny!

Tiny runs through the snow. The elf and I ride behind. *Wheee!* After a few wrong turns, we finally find the truck. Tiny is a big help.

We load the tree onto his back and return to the senior center.

Everyone cheers when they see we have the tree.

There is snow all over my boots, coat, and hat, so I take them off. Tiny wants the snow off, too. He quickly shakes his whole body.

Oh no! The nurse
is covered in snow.
Tiny is sorry again.

But this time, the
nurse doesn't get
mad. She just pats
Tiny and tells him
he's a good dog.

After warming up by the fire, we all decorate the tree together. It looks beautiful!

Merry Christmas, Tiny!